THE CHILDREN'S CLASSICS Collection

Volume 2

Dados Internacionais de Catalogação na Publicação (CIP) de acordo com ISBD

S772h Spyri, Johanna
Heidi / Johanna Spyri. - Jandira, SP : W. Books, 2025.
120 p. ; 12,80cm x 19,80cm - (Classics).

ISBN: 978-65-5294-112-1

1. Literatura suíça. 2. Clássicos. 3. Aventura. 4. Fantasia. 5. Imaginação. I. Título. II. Série.

2024-2498 CDD 849.4
CDU 82-494

Elaborada por Lucio Feitosa - CRB-8/8803
Índice para catálogo sistemático:
1. Literatura inglesa 849.4
2. Literatura inglesa 82-494

Text based on the original story by Johanna Spyri,
adapted by Catherine Veitch
Illustrations by Archina Laezza

1st edition in 2025
www.cirandacultural.com.br

Heidi

Johanna Spyri

W. Books

Heidi

An orphan

Aunt Deta

Heidi's aunt

Grandfather

Heidi's grandfather

Peter

A goatherd and Heidi's friend

Grandmother

Peter's grandmother

Clara
Heidi's friend
in Frankfurt

Mr Sesemann
Clara's father

Miss Rottenmeier
Mr Sesemann's
housekeeper

Grandmama
Clara's grandmother

Chapter One

One sunny June morning, Heidi and her Aunt Deta were walking along a narrow, winding path up the Alm Mountain.

Heidi was feeling cross. Despite the hot June weather, she was wearing two dresses, a red woollen shawl and thick mountain shoes.

'I could walk much faster if I wasn't wearing all these clothes,' Heidi complained.

'You'll need them at your grandfather's and I don't want to carry them,' her aunt told her. 'Besides, we'll be there soon.'

'Are you sure Grandfather will want me to stay with him?' Heidi asked nervously.

'I know he hasn't seen you since you were a baby, but he is family.

He can hardly turn you away.'

'But you've always said how miserable he is,' said Heidi.

'Well, maybe you'll cheer him up,' said Aunt Deta, not meeting her niece's eyes. 'Anyway, we're here now.'

Heidi looked up to see that they had reached a hut at the very top of the mountain. Aunt Deta knocked on the door. It creaked open and an old man peered out.

Heidi stared at him anxiously. He didn't look happy to see them.

'What do you want?' the old man grumbled.

'This is Heidi, your granddaughter,' Aunt Deta explained. 'Your dead son's child. You may not recognise her as you haven't seen her since she was one year old.'

'Hello, Grandfather,' said Heidi shyly, holding out her hand.

'Hmm ...' The old man roughly shook Heidi's hand and looked at her from under his bushy eyebrows.

'And you've brought her here because ...?'

'I've brought her here to live with you,' said Aunt Deta.

'Well, you can take her away again. I don't want her,' the old man said gruffly, trying to shut the door. Aunt Deta quickly wedged it open with her foot.

'I don't care,' she said. 'You have to take her. I've looked after her for four years, but now I've found

gruffly

In a way that lacks patience and seems unfriendly.

a good job in Frankfurt and I can't take her with me. So there's no choice, I'm afraid.'

Aunt Deta bent down and kissed Heidi. 'Be good,' she said. Then she turned and ran down the mountain. She did not look back.

Grandfather stared silently at Heidi. Heidi looked back with her big blue eyes, trying not to cry.

He doesn't want me, she thought. *But I have nowhere else to go.*

'Well,' said Grandfather, scowling at his granddaughter. 'You had better come inside.'

Chapter Two

The old man opened the door and Heidi stepped inside after him. She found herself in a large room, which covered the whole ground floor of the hut. The only furniture was a cupboard, a table and chair, and a bed in one corner. There was also a fire with a large kettle hanging above it. Heidi looked around carefully. There didn't seem to be any room left for her.

'Where am I to sleep?' she asked.

Her grandfather shrugged. 'Wherever you like.'

Heidi was delighted with this answer and immediately explored all the nooks and crannies to find the best place to sleep. In the corner, near her grandfather's bed, she saw a short ladder leaning against a wall. Wondering what was at the top, she climbed it and discovered a hayloft filled with fresh, sweet-smelling hay. Through a round window in the wall, she could see the green valley

far below and hear fir trees whooshing in the wind.

She smoothed some of the hay into the shape of a mattress.

'I shall sleep up here, Grandfather,' she called down the ladder. 'It's perfect. All I need is a blanket or two.'

'Well, at least the girl seems to have some sense,' Grandfather muttered to himself. 'Come down now,' he called. 'It's time for supper.'

Grandfather couldn't help but marvel at the small girl who bustled around his home as though she had always been there.

While he toasted a large piece of cheese on a long iron fork over the fire, Heidi ran back and forth to the cupboard, taking things out and putting them on the table. When the cheese was a delicious golden brown on each side, Heidi realised just how hungry she was.

Mouth-watering smells filled the air as Grandfather spread the melted cheese over a slice of bread for each of them, then filled their glasses with milk from his goats.

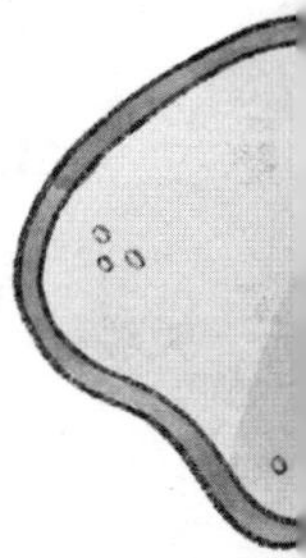

Heidi gobbled down chunks of bread oozing with cheese and drank the milk to the last drop.

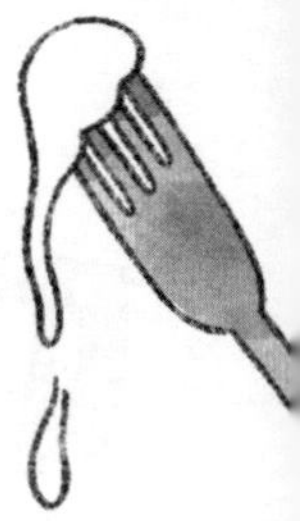

'Was that nice?' asked Grandfather, amused by his granddaughter's huge appetite.

‘I’ve never eaten or drunk anything as good as that before,’ said Heidi, smiling at him.

For the first time in a long while, Heidi’s grandfather gave a genuine smile.

That evening, Heidi and her grandfather watched through the open door as the sun slowly set behind the mountain, lighting the hut in a soft orange glow.

'I like it here, Grandfather,' said Heidi, smiling, before letting out a huge yawn. 'Will you tell me stories about my father and my grandmother?'

'Isn't it time you were in bed?' he asked bluntly, ignoring her question. The old man didn't like talking about the past. It was too painful for him.

Heidi climbed up the ladder into the hayloft. As she snuggled down under a blanket, surrounded by hay, she wondered why Grandfather lived all alone, high on the mountain. What had happened to him to make him so cross and unfriendly?

Chapter Three

Early the next morning, Heidi woke to the sound of bells. She sat up and looked around the hayloft. Sunshine poured in through the window, turning her straw bed into shimmering gold.

She dressed quickly and hurried down the ladder.

To her surprise, a boy who looked about ten or eleven years old stood at the door, humming to himself.

'This is Peter, the goatherd,' Grandfather told her. 'He's come for Little Swan and Little Bear.'

Just then, two goats – one white, one brown – pushed past him and sniffed Heidi's hand. She giggled as they licked her fingers.

'Their tongues tickle!' she laughed.

'Would you like to come with me?' Peter asked her. 'I'm going up the mountain to find fresh grass for them.'

'Can I, Grandfather?' Heidi

goatherd

A person who looks after a group of goats.

asked, her eyes shining. A day out on the mountain sounded like so much fun.

'Have your breakfast first,' Grandfather said, pulling up a stool and milking Little Bear. He handed Heidi a cup filled with fresh milk. 'Here.'

Heidi gulped down the milk. She didn't think she'd ever tasted anything so delicious.

'Come on,' Peter said, as Heidi wiped her mouth. 'You can stay at the back and make sure no goats wander off or get lost.'

'Be careful she doesn't fall over any rocks!' Grandfather shouted, as Peter and Heidi happily set off up the mountain.

'Why does Grandfather live all alone?' asked Heidi.

'I've no idea,' said Peter.

'Everyone says he's miserable,' said Heidi. 'But I don't know how anyone can be miserable living in a place like this.'

'He's always seemed okay to me,' said Peter.

As they set off over the rocks, Peter pointed out all the mountain's hidden secrets. He showed Heidi an eagle's nest tucked away in the craggy peaks and the spots where the wildflowers grew.

Heidi ran here and there, squealing with delight at seeing all the lovely flowers. The goats were as lively as Heidi, running in all directions, and Peter found it hard work to keep an eye on all of them at once.

Finally, they reached the meadow where Peter could leave his goats to graze. He lay down on the warm ground to rest. Heidi could not remember the last time she had felt so happy. She raised her chin so the golden sunlight hit her face, and breathed in the fresh mountain air and the sweet smell of the grass. She wished she could stay there forever.

When it was time for lunch, Peter opened a little package Heidi's grandfather had given him and placed the large pieces of bread and cheese on the paper.

Then he took a small bowl and milked Little Swan, so they had fresh milk to drink.

'What are the goats' names?' Heidi asked Peter.

'That's Hercules,' Peter said, pointing to a goat with big horns. 'He's always trying to headbutt the others. Only Greenfinch is brave enough to take him on.' Peter nodded towards a small, slim goat.

'And who is that?' Heidi asked, pointing to the white goat.

'That one there is White Snowflake.' At the sound of his name, White Snowflake let out

such a sad little bleat that Heidi ran straight over to stroke him.

Just then, Peter spotted the curious Greenfinch edging towards the side of the mountain where the rocks fell sharply below. Peter ran through the middle of the flock and threw himself on the ground, grabbing Greenfinch's back legs. Greenfinch bleated furiously and struggled to get loose. Heidi quickly gathered a bunch of sweet-smelling leaves and held them out to Greenfinch.

'Come on, Greenfinch, don't be so naughty!' she said.

The young goat turned around to eat the leaves out of Heidi's hand, and Peter was able to lead it away from the mountain's edge.

'That was good thinking,' said Peter, looking impressed. 'You'd make a good goatherd.'

Heidi blushed with pride.

It was soon time to go home.

Peter led Heidi, Little Swan and Little Bear back to her grandfather's house. The old man was waiting on a new swing that he had made and put up under the fir trees.

'Oh, Grandfather!' cried Heidi. 'Did you put that up for me?'

'I thought you might like to sit on it and look at the view,' he said, looking anywhere but at Heidi.

'Oh, thank you,' said Heidi, immediately sitting down and rocking herself back and forth. 'The mountain is so beautiful, especially the roses on the rocks and the blue and yellow flowers. I love it here.'

That night Heidi slept soundly on her bed of hay, dreaming of shining mountains covered with red roses.

Chapter Four

Peter arrived bright and early with his goats the next morning. Once again, the two children set off up the mountain to the meadow.

This went on day after day, until Heidi had spent so much time outdoors amongst the flowers and the grass that her cheeks had grown rosy and her eyes sparkled.

Every evening, she ate bread and cheese and drank milk in front of the fire, while Grandfather told her stories. But no matter how much Heidi begged him to talk about her family, he always refused.

When autumn came, the wind blew strong and loud. Grandfather told Heidi she had to stay at home. 'A sudden gust of the wind could blow a little thing like you over the rocks and into the valley below,' he said.

Heidi missed Peter and the goats, but she made sure to see him every day when he dropped off Little Swan and Little Bear.

‘The goats are much naughtier when you’re not around,’ Peter told her.

As winter drew in, the weather got colder. One night there was a heavy fall of snow, and the next morning the whole mountain was covered in a blanket of pure white.

Heidi and her grandfather were huddled in front of the fire, when there was a loud thump on the door. It was Peter, covered head to foot in snow.

‘Come inside and get warm,’ Grandfather told him.

Peter didn’t need to be asked

twice. Shivering, he hurried inside and held his hands out in front of the fire.

'Would you like something to eat?' Heidi asked.

'If that's okay?' Peter said, looking at Grandfather.

The old man nodded. 'We have plenty to go around.'

Peter's eyes widened when Grandfather gave him a large piece of meat on a thick slice of bread.

'My grandmother asked if you would like to come and visit,' Peter said, between mouthfuls of meat and bread.

'I'd love to,' said Heidi. 'I'll come tomorrow.'

The next day, Heidi knocked on Peter's grandmother's door.

'Come in,' called a voice.

Heidi hurried inside. An old blind woman sat at a spinning wheel. 'Who is there?' she asked.

'I'm Heidi, Peter's friend. I have come to see you,' replied Heidi.

The old woman smiled in Heidi's direction. 'I'm so pleased to meet you. Peter has told me so much about you.'

As the two of them chatted, Heidi looked around the room. It was small and bare, and all the furniture had seen better days. Despite a fire burning away merrily in the corner, it was cold inside. She jumped as one of the shutters banged in the wind. It had come loose from the wall.

'One of your shutters is broken,' Heidi said. 'My grandfather could fix it for you.'

'Dear child,' the old woman said, smiling. 'Everything in this old place rattles and creaks when the wind blows. The cold gets inside through all the cracks and holes.'

'Don't worry,' said Heidi. 'Grandfather will be able to fix it.'

As soon as she got home, Heidi told Grandfather all about Peter's grandmother's house.

'We should definitely do

something to help,' said Grandfather. 'I will go round tomorrow and do whatever I can.'

Heidi jumped up and gave Grandfather a huge hug.

'Thank you, Grandfather,' she said, smiling up at him. She hardly recognised him from the gruff and grumpy man she had first met. Heidi loved him with all her heart.

Chapter Five

By the time Heidi was eight years old, she had learnt many things from living on the mountain with her grandfather. She knew how to look after goats, how to whistle like Peter, and how to toast cheese until it was a delicious, bubbling golden brown. Little Swan and Little Bear followed her around like two faithful dogs, which made Grandfather smile. Heidi had never been happier.

Then, one sunny March morning, the door flew open and there stood Aunt Deta. She wore a pretty feathered hat and a long trailing dress that swept the floor.

'I've come for Heidi,' she announced. 'I should never have left her here in the first place.'

'No!' cried Heidi. 'I like it here with Grandfather!'

Aunt Deta ignored her. 'I've

found a place for Heidi with a rich family in Frankfurt,' she said to Grandfather. 'Clara Sesemann is a little girl who's very unwell and needs a companion. Mr Sesemann will pay for Heidi's service and buy her new clothes. It's a great chance for her.'

Grandfather, who had been

companion

A person who is employed to keep someone company.

looking crosser and crosser during this speech, shook his head. 'Give your job to someone else,' he said. 'I will not hear of it.'

'This is a good chance for her,' repeated Aunt Deta. 'It's better than being stuck on this mountain forever.'

Grandfather's eyes flashed with anger. 'Look at you, with your fancy clothes. You think you're better than us, don't you?'

With that, he strode out of the house. Heidi watched through the window as he walked away up the mountain, rubbing the back of his head with his hand.

Aunt Deta hurried around the house, picking up Heidi's clothes and stuffing them into a pillowcase. Then she grabbed Heidi by the arm.

'I'm not going with you,' Heidi said, trying to pull away.

'Don't be so silly,' said Aunt Deta, dragging a protesting Heidi towards the door. 'This is the right thing. Even your grandfather knows that.'

As her aunt dragged her towards the mountain path, Heidi glanced back over her shoulder.

Her grandfather was sitting on the swing under the fir tree, his face buried in his arms.

'Poor Grandfather!' Heidi said, tears rolling down her face. 'He will be lonely without me.'

'He won't even notice you're gone,' muttered her aunt. 'I should never have left you with that cross old man.'

'He's not cross,' Heidi cried, 'he's sad. I wish I understood why he is so sad.'

'He's sad because he thinks the world is a bad place,' Aunt Deta said. 'First his wife died, and then his son. He pushed away everyone else, until he lost them too.'

Heidi's heart broke for her grandfather. No wonder he had seemed so miserable when she had first met him. He had lost everyone he loved.

'He hasn't pushed me away,' she cried. 'But now he's losing me too, and it's all your fault.'

'Don't you dare speak to me like that, young lady. You need to think about your future,' scolded Aunt Deta. 'Forget about your grandfather.'

'I'll never forget him,' whispered Heidi. And she made a promise to herself, right there and then, that one day she would come back to her grandfather.

The journey to Frankfurt was long and tiring. By the time Heidi and Aunt Deta stopped outside a big house in a cobbled street, it was early evening.

'Be on your best behaviour,' Aunt Deta told Heidi as she pulled the bell.

The door opened and a well-dressed servant led them into a grand hallway. Heidi felt very scruffy in her plain woollen dress and straw hat. She felt even worse when Miss Rottenmeier, the housekeeper, saw her.

‘You look most unsuitable,’ the housekeeper said, letting out a disappointed sigh.

Heidi wasn’t sure how to reply to this, so she decided not to say anything.

'Can you read, young lady?' Miss Rottenmeier asked.

'I have not learnt to read yet,' replied Heidi.

'What have you learnt then?' said Miss Rottenmeier.

'Nothing!' answered Heidi, truthfully. 'Apart from how to herd the goats on my grandfather's mountain.'

Miss Rottenmeier turned to Aunt Deta. 'This is not at all the sort of companion we want. How could you bring a child like this here?'

Aunt Deta lifted her chin.

'Heidi is absolutely perfect for this position. She knows a lot about flowers and has a lot of energy.'

'Hmm,' said Miss Rottenmeier, who didn't seem at all convinced. 'Well, I suppose you better meet Clara.'

She led Heidi into the vast dining room, where a young girl was sitting on a chair. She looked pale and tired.

Miss Rottenmeier sat beside the girl. 'This is Clara,' she said. Heidi sat on a chair and smiled at Clara.

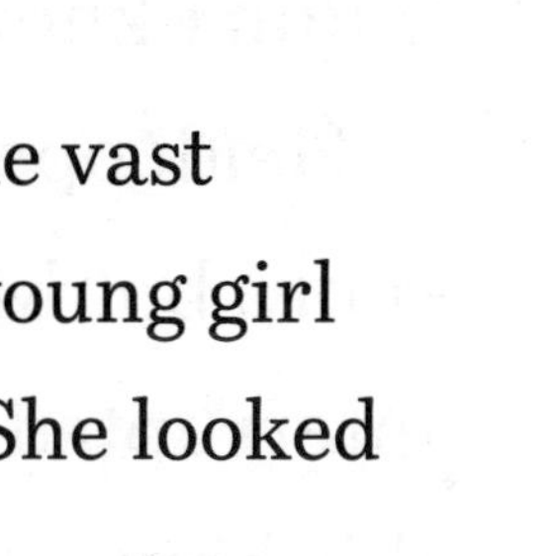

‘Pleased to meet you,’ she said.

‘Thank you for coming,’ Clara said quietly. ‘I’ll like having company. I can’t do very much.’

‘Why not?’ asked Heidi.

‘I’ve been sick,’ Clara explained. ‘I don’t know if I’ll ever get better.’

Heidi opened her mouth to reply, but Miss Rottenmeier interrupted. ‘If you are to live in this house, then there are rules you must follow,’ she told Heidi. ‘Never speak to the servants unless you have an order to give them – they are not your friends. I expect you to …’

Heidi's eyes began to droop. It had been a long, exhausting day, and as she leant back in her chair, she fell asleep.

'Do you understand, child?' asked Miss Rottenmeier, who had finally finished her lecture.

Clara giggled. 'Heidi is fast asleep, Miss Rottenmeier,' she said. She had not had such a fun dinner for a long time.

Chapter Six

When Heidi woke up the next morning, she could not remember where she was. She jumped out of bed, threw on her clothes and ran to the window. She wanted to see the sky and the green grass

outside, but instead there were brick walls and cobbles. The street below was crowded with people, horses and carriages.

'It's so different from the mountain!' Heidi breathed, trying to take in all the strange sights, smells and sounds.

Tearing herself away from the view, Heidi hurried downstairs for breakfast. Miss Rottenmeier appeared as she was finishing her last mouthful.

'Stop dawdling over breakfast, child,' she said. 'Clara's tutor is here. I expect lessons to start on time in this house.'

Miss Rottenmeier led Heidi to the study. The room was quiet and cosy, filled with various things standing and lying about, a large bookcase with glass doors, comfortable sofas and two desks. Clara was already sitting at one

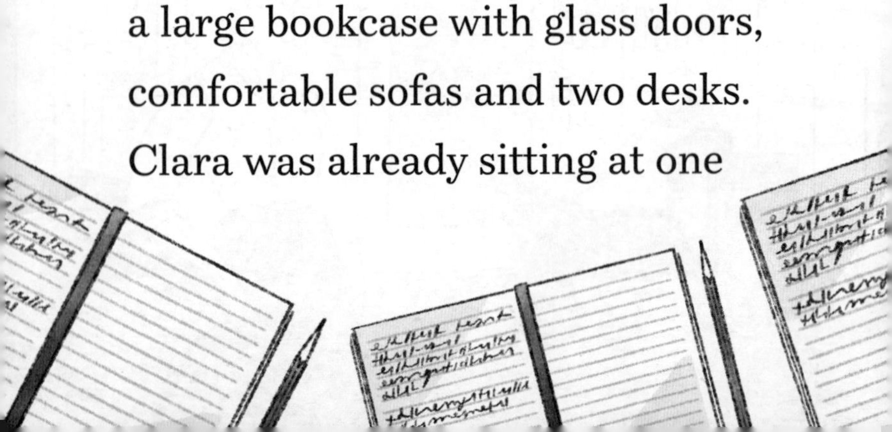

of the desks, while a young man was setting up some books on the other.

'I'm afraid this child still has a lot to learn, timekeeping included,' the housekeeper said to the tutor. 'She is extremely uneducated.'

The tutor smiled kindly at Heidi. 'I have no doubt that the child may be behind in some areas, but she will be ahead in others. The two girls can help each other to learn.'

He nodded at the desk next to Clara, and Heidi hurried over to sit down. As she did, a carriage passed by the window, making her jump and knock over some ink. She watched in horror as a dark stream of ink ran across the tablecloth and onto the floor.

'It wasn't Heidi's fault,' said Clara quickly.

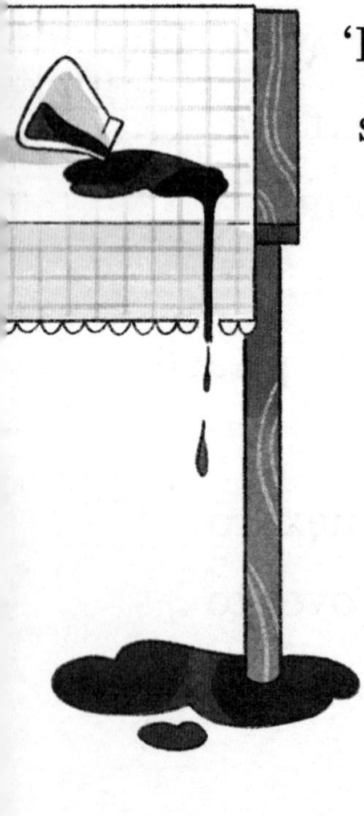

'I don't think she's ever seen or heard carriages before. Please don't punish her.'

There was nothing Miss Rottenmeier could do. She had to obey Clara.

She sighed loudly

and rolled her eyes. ‘I will excuse you this time,’ she told Heidi crossly. ‘But if you do it again, there will be trouble.’

Heidi stared down at the desk, trying not to cry.

‘Tell me about the mountains,’ Clara said kindly. ‘I want to hear all about your home. It sounds wonderful.’

‘It is,’ Heidi said. ‘I miss the fresh air and running through the meadows with Peter and the goats. But most of all, I miss Grandfather. Everything’s so different here.’

Clara looked sad. 'Since I've been ill, I can't walk, let alone run.'

'That's terrible,' said Heidi, Detarmined to do everything she could to make Clara feel better.

The next morning, Miss Rottenmeier told Heidi that Clara was too ill to get out of bed.

'I'll go and see her,' said Heidi.

Clara lay on a heap of pillows in a huge four-poster bed. Her face was pale and the room was hot.

'Thanks for coming to see me,' Clara said. 'I feel too weak to get out of bed. Sometimes I don't think I'll ever get better.'

'Your room's so warm,' said Heidi. 'Why don't I open the window and let some air in? We always had the windows open whenever we could at Grandfather's.' She ran over to the window and flung it open.

Leaning out, she saw a ragged boy playing a street organ. A pair of cute kittens were peeking out of his pockets. Watching him, Heidi had an idea.

'I'll be right back,' she told Clara excitedly.

Heidi rushed downstairs and into the street. 'Can you come here?' she called to the boy. 'There's someone I'd love you to play for.'

'Surprise!' Heidi shouted a few moments later, throwing Clara's door open and pushing the boy inside. Moments later, music, singing, laughter and the mewing of kittens floated out of the room.

'Whatever is going on?' Miss Rottenmeier shrieked, as she hurried into the room. 'How ever did this dreadful boy get inside

this house?' she cried. 'Explain yourself!' She glared at Heidi.

'She was only trying to cheer me up,' said Clara.

Miss Rottenmeier wasn't listening. 'I have had more than enough of you and your trouble-making ways!' she shouted at Heidi. 'Go to your room at once.'

But Clara gripped Heidi's hands. 'I want Heidi to stay here,' she said. 'We want to have lunch together.'

'As you wish,' Miss Rottenmeier said reluctantly. 'But get that dirty boy out of here now. And make sure he takes those filthy kittens with him.'

With that, she flounced out of the room.

Heidi and Clara thanked the boy and kissed the kittens goodbye.

'I wish I could keep you,' Heidi said sadly. 'I miss having animals.'

Miss Rottenmeier returned shortly after, carrying a tray piled high with dishes.

'Here is your lunch,' she told the girls. 'Tuck in.'

Heidi looked at the food and sighed. Chunks of meat swam in a rich cream sauce. She missed the

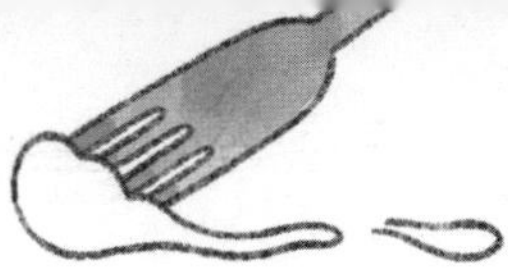
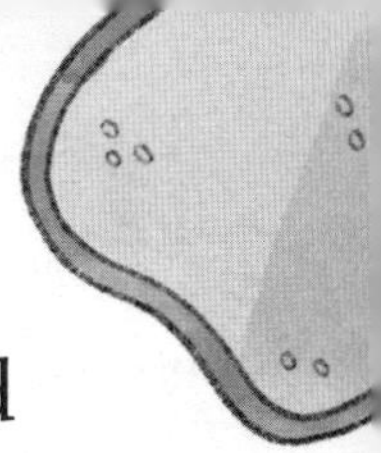

simple lunches of cheese, bread and fresh milk she had eaten every day on the mountain. Clara didn't seem to like it much either. She pushed it around her plate and hardly ate anything.

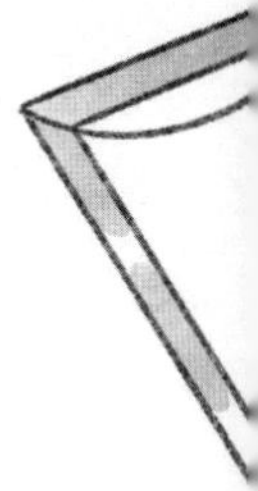

'I don't get very hungry lying in bed or just sitting in my chair,' she muttered.

'I was always hungry in the mountains,' Heidi told her. 'I seem to have lost my appetite here.' She longed for the cool clear air of the mountains and the soft breeze that made the fir trees rustle.

As the days passed by, Heidi felt more and more homesick. She missed Grandfather, Peter and the goats desperately. So, one day, she packed up some rolls from the dinner table in her red shawl – they would make a lovely treat for Peter's grandmother – then put on her red hat and made her way to the front door.

'Where do you think you're going?' asked Miss Rottenmeier.

'Home,' said Heidi. 'I miss the goats. And Grandfather will be missing me.'

'Have you lost your mind, child?' the housekeeper cried. 'You can't just leave whenever you feel like it.'

She grabbed Heidi's arm and pulled her towards the stairs. Heidi stumbled and dropped her shawl. Miss Rottenmeier gasped as the bread rolls fell out and rolled across the carpet.

'Throw those away at once,' she ordered.

'They're for Peter's grandmother,' cried Heidi, bursting into tears. 'Please let me keep them!'

Clara wheeled her chair into the hallway to see what was going on. 'Don't cry, Heidi,' she said softly, moving towards Heidi and placing her arm around her waist kindly. 'I promise you can take all the bread rolls you like when you go home. I'll give them to you myself.'

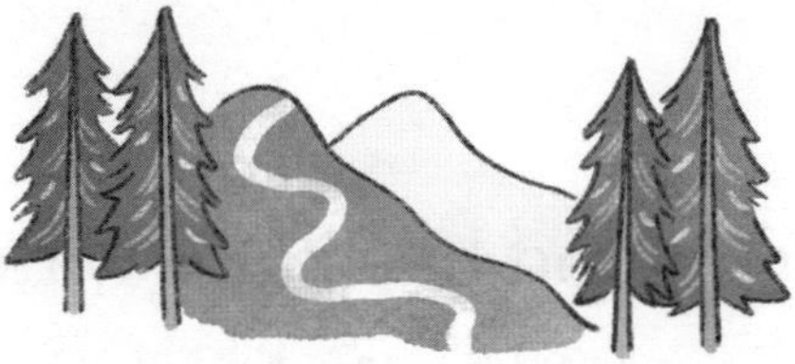

Chapter Seven

A few days later, the house was buzzing with activity. Clara's father, Mr Sesemann, had returned, and the servants were busy carrying packages up and down the stairs. He had brought back as many lovely things as he could find for his daughter.

Clara was overjoyed to see her father. The two of them were very close and she had missed him desperately.

Heidi stood back and watched as Clara and her father hugged. She could see how emotional they both were, and it made her miss her grandfather even more. Clara looked up at her and smiled. 'Father, I'd like you to meet Heidi,' she said, holding out her hand towards Heidi. 'She's been keeping me company and has become a really good friend.'

Mr Sesemann stood up from where he was kneeling next to his daughter and looked at Heidi. 'Any friend of my daughter is a friend of

mine,' he said. 'I'm very pleased to meet you, Heidi.'

Heidi shyly shook hands with Clara's father. 'I hope Clara has been treating you well,' he said. As he smiled, Heidi noticed the lines around his eyes crinkle.

'She's one of the kindest people I've ever met,' Heidi said truthfully.

'I'm glad to hear it,' said Mr Sesemann. 'Kindness is often underrated. Now, you two go and find something to do while I find Miss Rottenmeier.'

underrated
Not valued enough.

He found the housekeeper in the dining room.

'I've just met Heidi,' he told her.

'I was hoping for a well-behaved, nicely brought up little girl,' she said. 'But I'm afraid Heidi has turned out to be quite the opposite. The whole house has been in chaos since she arrived.'

'She seemed like a perfectly normal child of her age to me,' replied Mr Sesemann.

'Appearances can be deceptive,' Miss Rottenmeier replied sharply. 'I knew she was trouble from the moment I saw her. She's ruined a

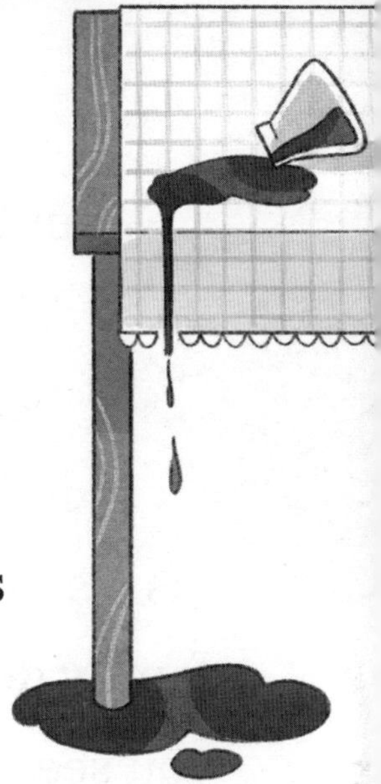

tablecloth with ink, stolen food and tried to run away. I think you should send her home.'

'Let's see what Clara has to say,' Mr Sesemann said, calling for his daughter. 'Miss Rottenmeier has told me there's been some problems with Heidi,' he said gently, as Clara wheeled into the room. 'What's been happening? I heard she stole some food.'

'Heidi has only ever tried to cheer me up,' Clara said, glaring at Miss Rottenmeier. 'She's really funny and incredibly thoughtful.

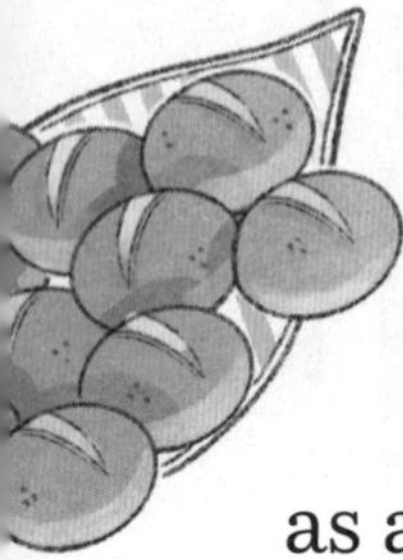

She only took the bread because she wanted to give it to her friend's grandmother as a special treat. Her friend's family don't have much money, you see.'

'It sounds like you don't want me to send Heidi away,' he said.

'Please don't!' Clara cried. 'It used to be so boring and dull here. But time passes so much quicker since Heidi arrived. Something different happens every day. And I love hearing her stories about the mountains.'

'Then it's agreed,' Mr Sesemann said. 'There'll be no more talk of Heidi leaving.'

As Miss Rottenmeier tutted loudly and stalked out of the room, muttering to herself, Mr Sesemann winked at his daughter. 'Your grandmama is arriving in a few days,' he said. 'Something tells me that she and this Heidi of yours are going to get on like a house on fire.'

Heidi liked Grandmama straight away. There was something kind and warm-hearted about the old lady. She especially liked the picture books that Grandmama had brought with her for Clara.

'There's no point giving that to her,' Miss Rottenmeier said, when Grandmama handed one of the books to Heidi. 'The girl can't even read properly.'

'The pictures are beautiful though,' said Heidi, flipping through the pages.

'It's yours to keep,' Grandmama said to Heidi. 'And we can learn to read it together.'

Every day, Heidi sat with Grandmama and the two of them read the book together.

Soon, Heidi was able to read it all by herself.

'I can't thank you enough for teaching me,' Heidi said.

Grandmama looked over to where Clara was sitting in a chair, looking happier than she had ever seen her.

'I think it's you who is teaching us,' Grandmama answered.

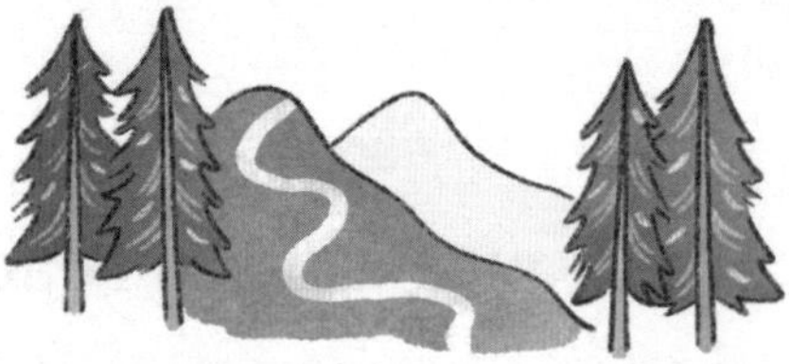

Chapter Eight

The servants in Mr Sesemann's house were very upset. They were convinced that there was a ghost haunting the house.

'Every night a white figure floats down the stairs,' one of them told Miss Rottenmeier.

The housekeeper decided she had no choice but to tell Mr Sesemann.

'There's no such thing as ghosts,' he laughed.

'Try telling the servants that,' Miss Rottenmeier said. 'It's no joke in their eyes.'

'Fine,' Mr Sesemann said. 'I'll stay up all night and catch your supposed ghost.'

That night, he waited in the hall at the bottom of the stairs, but there was no sign of the ghost.

Just as he was about to give up, he caught sight of something white out of the corner of his eye. He crept towards the stairs. As the moonlight shone in through the hall window, it fell on a small white figure floating down the stairs. He watched the ghost glide towards the front door and try to open it.

'Heidi?' Mr Sesemann called, realising who the 'ghost' was.

The girl turned and let out a small cry. 'What's happening?' she asked, looking around in confusion. 'Why aren't I in bed?'

Mr Sesemann hurried over and put his arm around her. 'You were sleepwalking,' he told her. 'Let's get you back to bed.'

As they climbed the stairs, Mr Sesemann asked Heidi if she could remember what she was dreaming about.

'Oh yes,' said Heidi. 'I have the same dream every night. I'm back with Grandfather on the mountain. I hear the fir trees outside, and I can see the stars in the night sky shining so brightly through the window. It's all so beautiful that I can't stop myself from running outside. But when I wake, I'm always by your front door.' She started to cry. 'I don't know what's wrong with me.'

‘You’re going to be fine,’ Mr Sesemann said, tucking Heidi in before sitting on the side of her bed. ‘You are obviously homesick and missing your grandfather dearly. There’s only one cure I can think of.’

‘What is it?’ sobbed Heidi, feeling even more miserable at the thought of being given some horrible-tasting medicine.

‘You must go home and see your grandfather at once,’ Mr Sesemann told her, grinning as a delighted Heidi flung her arms around him.

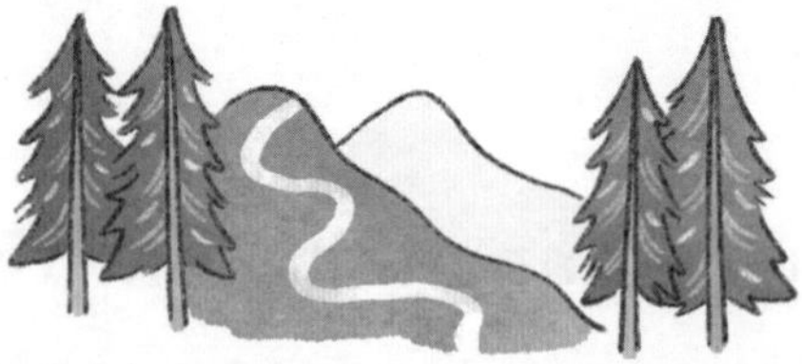

Chapter Nine

The very next morning, Mr Sesemann saw to it that a large trunk was crammed to the brim with new dresses, aprons and handkerchiefs for Heidi to take with her. Heidi stared at the clothes in amazement. She had never seen so much finery. She carefully placed the picture book that

Grandmama had given her on top of the garments. Peter wouldn't recognise her.

'These are for Peter's grandmother,' said Clara, holding out a basket filled with the most delicious-smelling fresh rolls.

'You didn't forget!' cried Heidi.

'Of course not,' said Clara, smiling. 'I just wish I could come with you. But Father and the doctor both say that I'm too ill to travel right now.'

'But you will visit us soon?' asked Heidi. 'I want to show you the mountain.'

‘As soon as I’m allowed,’ said Clara. ‘I can’t wait to meet Peter and his grandmother, and your grandfather too.’

At the thought of her beloved grandfather, Heidi couldn’t stop grinning. She couldn’t wait to see the look on his face when she returned home.

Heidi couldn’t stop smiling as she climbed up the steep path from the town. She had thought she would never see the beautiful mountain again, and yet here she was. She kept stopping to catch her breath as the basket she carried was heavy.

At last, Heidi caught the familiar sight of Peter's house in the hollow of the craggy rock, and her heart beat so fast that she thought it might fly right out of her chest and zoom around the mountain.

'Who is there?' came a voice, as Heidi knocked on the door.

'It's me!' cried Heidi. She ran inside and flung herself on her knees beside the old woman.

'Heidi! Is that really you?' asked Peter's grandmother, stroking Heidi's curly hair as happy tears fell from her unseeing eyes.

'Yes, it's me! I've come back for good!' Heidi cried. 'And I've got a present for you, all the way from Frankfurt!' Heidi grabbed the twelve rolls from her basket and piled them onto the old woman's lap.

'Fresh bread!' gasped Peter's grandmother. 'It smells so good.'

'Don't even think of letting Peter eat them all,' said Heidi, grinning.

Peter's grandmother laughed. 'He's going to be so very excited to see you!'

'I know, and I can't wait to see him either. But first, I must go home to Grandfather. I can't wait to see his face.'

Heidi said goodbye and continued walking up the mountain. She couldn't help but think about the first time she'd walked along the path with her Aunt Deta. She'd been so scared and worried that her grandfather wouldn't want her. And now, all she wanted was to stay there forever.

Finally, she saw the tops of the fir trees above Grandfather's little wooden house. And there, sitting on the very same swing where she'd last seen him all that time before, was her grandfather. Heidi began to run faster and faster. She raced up the slope and threw herself into his arms.

'Heidi!' he cried. 'You've come home at last!'

'I missed you so much,' Heidi sobbed happily.

‘I didn’t think I’d ever see you again,’ Grandfather whispered, holding her tightly.

Hand in hand, the two of them walked back into the house. Heidi looked around at the familiar furniture and the fire roaring in the corner.

That night, Grandfather made a cosy bed for Heidi in the hayloft, and Heidi had the best sleep since she had last left the mountain.

Chapter Ten

After a long, hard winter, Heidi was excited when spring finally arrived and the mountain turned green again. The days were warmer and lighter, the air was full of delicious, sweet scents, and wildflowers were blossoming and blooming everywhere Heidi looked.

One day, Heidi was perched on the swing, looking down the mountain, when the strangest sight caught her eye. She blinked, rubbed her eyes and looked again. The most peculiar procession was making its way up the mountain slope.

Two men were struggling with large trunks. A third was holding a wheelchair, and a fourth was carefully carrying a child wrapped up in a shawl. The men puffed and panted, their shirts drenched in sweat. Behind them strode a familiar elderly woman.

procession

A group of people moving forward in a line.

'Grandfather, come quickly!' Heidi shouted, jumping off the swing and dancing around in excitement. 'It's Clara and Grandmama!'

Grandfather hurried outside as the procession finally arrived at the house, and Heidi ran to hug her visitors.

'I'm very pleased to meet you,' he said to Grandmama, before turning to Clara. 'Thank you for coming. You'll soon feel better breathing our fresh mountain air.'

'What a magnificent home you have!' Grandmama said. 'And

Heidi, you look so well. What do you think, Clara?'

Heidi wheeled Clara's chair round so that she could see the wonderful view. 'Oh Grandmama,' sighed Clara, gazing around her at the mountain. 'I would like to stay here forever.'

'Look!' Heidi said. 'There are the fir trees I told you about. Aren't they pretty?'

'I've never seen anything like it!' breathed Clara. 'They're so different from the trees we have in Frankfurt.'

‘You must be tired after your journey,’ said Grandfather. ‘Come inside.’

Clara and Grandmama sat at the table while Grandfather poured them all a bowl of fresh milk.

‘I’ve never tasted anything so delicious,’ said Grandmama, drinking thirstily.

‘It tastes so much nicer than the milk we have at home,’ added Clara, finishing hers.

‘This is where your milk came from,’ Heidi said, grinning as she led Little Swan into the room.

The goat gently butted Clara with her nose until she gave her a stroke. 'I wish we had goats,' she told Heidi.

Grandmama was looking around the room. 'Do I remember you telling me you sleep in the hayloft?' she asked.

'Yes, up there!' said Heidi, pointing to the ladder that led up to her bedroom. 'Would you like to see?'

'Yes please!' cried Clara.

Grandfather stood, scooped Clara up in his arms and carefully carried her up the ladder. Heidi scrambled up behind them as Grandfather set Clara down on the hay next to the window.

'I'll leave you two to catch up,' he said.

Clara gasped as she looked out of the hayloft window. 'You can look from your bed straight into the sky and hear the fir trees rustling!' said Clara. 'I have never seen such a happy bedroom before.'

'I know!' Heidi smiled at her friend. 'It's the most perfect place in the world.'

Grandfather poked his head into the hayloft again. 'Clara, your grandmother and I have been talking. We've agreed that you should stay here with us while your grandmother stays in the village. We think that being up here on the mountain will give you new strength and help you recover from your illness. I hope that's okay with you?'

Clara clapped her hands in delight, as Heidi leapt across the hay to hug her grandfather.

'This is the best day ever!' she cried.

Chapter Eleven

The next day, Peter arrived as usual to collect the goats.

'Come on, Heidi!' he called.

'I can't come,' Heidi answered. 'I have to stay with Clara.'

Peter threw Clara a jealous look.

'You go, Heidi,' Clara insisted. 'I'll be fine here. Grandfather will look after me.'

'Of course I will,' Grandfather said, smiling at Clara.

'Are you sure?' asked Heidi.

'Absolutely,' said Clara.

'I'll pick you some flowers and bring them back for you,' Heidi said, hugging her friend before skipping off after Peter. 'I won't be long!' she called over her shoulder.

When she glanced back, she couldn't help but notice the look of longing on her friend's face. Heidi felt bad. She knew Clara would do anything to be able to run and jump and skip over the mountain paths and meadows.

As she watched an eagle soar high above their heads, she

wished her friend could be with her. She picked the prettiest flowers she could find, then called over to Peter.

'I'm going to head home. I feel bad leaving Clara on her own.'

As she hurried away, Peter watched her with narrowed eyes. 'I wish that girl hadn't come. Heidi's *my* friend,' he muttered to himself. And a plan started to form in his mind as to how he could get rid of Clara.

The next morning, Peter crept to Grandfather's house. It was early, and everything was quiet and still. Clara's wheelchair stood outside the front door.

Peter glanced around to make sure no one was in sight, then he grabbed the chair. He pushed it to the top of the path, then let go. He watched it roll down the slope, faster and faster, until it hit a rock, flew into the air and crashed down onto the earth, smashing into a hundred pieces. Peter looked at what he had done and fled before anyone saw.

'Where is Clara's chair, Grandfather?' Heidi called, a few moments later. 'It's not in its usual place.'

'That's strange,' said Grandfather. 'It was definitely there last night.'

The pair searched all around the outside of the house, until Heidi let out a gasp and pointed down the path. 'Look!' she cried. 'The wind must have blown the chair down the path. And now it's completely broken. What are we going to do?'

'Don't worry,' Grandfather said. 'I can carry Clara wherever she needs to go. I wonder where Peter has got to. He's usually here by this time.'

Half an hour later, when Peter still hadn't appeared, Grandfather carried Clara up to the meadow. Heidi followed behind, a goat on either side. They were surprised to find Peter already there with the rest of the goats.

Heidi started telling Peter about what had happened to the wheelchair, as Grandfather gently lowered Clara onto a blanket on the ground.

'So, Clara will have to go home,' said Peter, looking at her with satisfaction.

'Aha,' said Grandfather, raising his eyebrows. 'I understand now.'

'What do you mean?' asked Heidi, confused.

'Peter?' asked Grandfather. 'Would you like to tell us what really happened to the chair?'

'I'm sorry,' Peter said, blushing. 'I wanted Clara to leave. Heidi doesn't have time for me anymore.'

'I never meant to make you feel

like that!' cried Clara. 'You must hate me, Peter.'

'I'm friends with both of you,' said Heidi. 'There's no need to dislike Clara. You would love her as much as me if you bothered to get to know her.'

'I really am sorry,' said Peter. 'I just didn't think.'

'No, you didn't,' said Grandfather. 'And I don't know how we're going to explain this to Mr Sesemann. I better go and see if there's any way of repairing it.'

Peter wanted to try and make it up to Clara and went to pick her some flowers. He found a spot where the whole ground shimmered gold as the wildflowers spread their yellow blossoms. He turned round and ran back to the girls.

'Heidi, Clara, you must come!' he called. 'It's more beautiful than you can imagine.'

'But we don't have my chair,' said Clara.

'We'll carry you,' said Peter.

Together, Heidi and Peter tried to lift Clara, but they weren't as strong as Grandfather.

'Let me try and walk,' said Clara. 'I've been feeling stronger than ever since I've been here.'

'Okay,' said Heidi. 'But be careful. Grandmama will never forgive me if you fall and hurt yourself.'

Peter and Heidi supported Clara under her arms, as Clara slowly put her feet on the ground.

'Steady now,' said Peter.

Taking a deep breath, Clara slowly put her weight on to one trembling foot and then the other. Peter and Heidi grinned at each other in amazement.

'I'm walking!' Clara gasped, tears of joy streaming down her face.

‘I’m actually walking!’

‘Rest now,’ Heidi said. ‘You can try again tomorrow.’

The three of them sank to the floor, laughing in delight and disbelief.

‘I’m going to practise every single day,’ said Clara. ‘Won’t Father be amazed?’

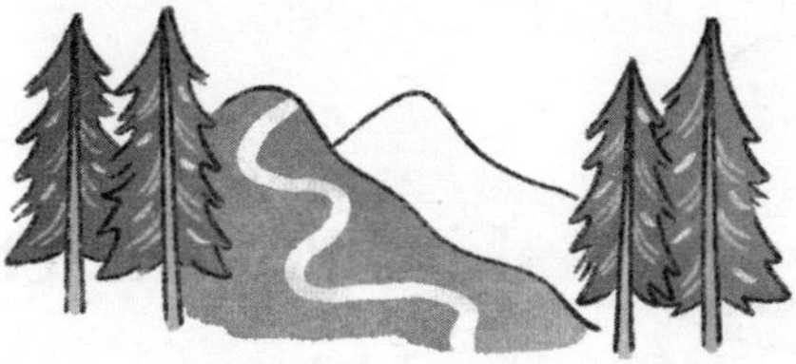

Chapter Twelve

Every day, Clara walked a little more. Hungry from the exercise and fresh air, she wolfed down huge meals. Strength flowed through her, and she tingled with energy.

Grandmama could not believe the incredible change. 'We have so much to thank you for,' she told Heidi and Grandfather.

'It's the mountain air you should be thanking,' laughed Grandfather. 'It truly works miracles.'

Little Swan let out a loud bleat.

'And don't forget the goat's milk,' added Heidi, as they all burst into laughter.

'I will send a telegram to Clara's father in Paris to tell him to get here at once,' said Grandmama.

'But don't tell him I can walk,' said Clara. 'I really want to surprise him.'

'It's going to be the best surprise ever,' said Heidi, hugging her friend. 'I can't wait to see his face.'

telegram

A written message sent using an electric device and then printed out onto paper.

But what none of them knew was that Mr Sesemann was making his way up the mountain at that very moment.

As Clara's father reached the very top of the mountain, he saw Heidi and Clara sitting outside the house on the swing. He hardly recognised his daughter with her rosy cheeks, glowing face and shining hair.

'Clara?' he called.

'Father!' she cried.

Mr Sesemann watched in disbelief as his daughter stood up from the swing and walked towards him, Heidi dancing behind her.

‘You can walk?’ he gasped. ‘You can really walk!’

‘Isn’t it amazing!’ laughed Clara. ‘Heidi made it happen.’

‘And Peter,’ added Grandfather, who had come out with Grandmama to see what all the commotion was.

‘You did it all by yourself,’ Heidi told Clara.

‘It’s a miracle,’ said Mr Sesemann, watching his daughter with tears in his eyes. ‘I can’t believe it. Thank you. Thank you all.’

Later that day, the friends and family all gathered inside Grandfather’s house.

'I can never repay you for all you have done,' said Mr Sesemann. 'How can I show you how grateful I am?'

'We don't need anything,' said Heidi. 'We have everything we could want right here.'

'But there must be something,' said Mr Sesemann.

'There is one thing,' said Grandfather.

'Anything. Just name it.'

'I am growing old. And I will not be here forever. It would make me happy to know that when I'm gone you will look after

Heidi, so she is never without a home.'

'It would be my pleasure,' said Mr Sesemann. 'Your granddaughter is already like a daughter to me. And I know Clara thinks of her as a sister.'

Clara smiled. 'The best of sisters.'

That night Heidi and Grandfather sat outside their house, gazing out at the view. The sun was setting and the mountain glowed pink-gold.

'It's beautiful,' sighed Heidi. 'It's just like the first evening

I arrived here all those years ago.'

'I was sad and lonely then,' said Grandfather, smiling at his granddaughter. 'But you have made me happy again.'

'We've made each other happy,' said Heidi. 'And we'll never be lonely again.'

Johanna Spyri

Johanna Spyri was born in a Swiss village with beautiful views of the Alps in 1827. Her father was a doctor and her mother was a poet. Throughout her childhood, Spyri wrote poetry and enjoyed being in nature. She was a very private person, so not much is known about her life. *Heidi* is her most famous book and was originally published in two parts in 1880 and 1881.